This book belongs to:

....

....

Retold by Gaby Goldsack
Illustrated by Kim Blundell (John Martin & Artists)
Language consultant: Betty Root

This edition published by Parragon in 2009

Parragon
Queen Street House
4 Queen Street
Bath BA1 1HE, UK

Copyright © Parragon Books Ltd 2002

ISBN 978-1-4075-0653-1

Printed in China

The Three Billy Goats Gruff

Bath New York Singapore Hong Kong Cologne Delhi Melbourne

Notes for Parents

These **Gold Stars**® reading books encourage and support children who are learning to read.

Starting to read

• Start by reading the book aloud to your child. Take time to talk about the pictures. They often give clues about the story. The easy-to-read speech bubbles provide an excellent 'joining-in' activity.

• Over time, try to read the same book several times. Gradually, your child will want to read the book aloud with you. It helps to run your finger under the words as you say them.

• Occasionally, stop and encourage your child to continue reading aloud without you. Join in again when your child needs help. This is the next step towards helping your child become an independent reader.

• Finally, your child will be ready to read alone. Listen carefully and give plenty of praise. Remember to make reading an enjoyable experience.

Using your stickers
The fun colour stickers in the centre of the book and fold-out scene board at the back will help your child re-enact parts of the story, again and again.

Remember these four stages:
• Read the story **to** your child.

• Read the story **with** your child.

• Encourage your child to read **to you.**

• Listen to your child read **alone.**

Once upon a time there were three
Billy Goats Gruff.

There was a big Billy Goat Gruff.

There was a middle-sized Billy Goat Gruff.

And there was a little Billy Goat Gruff.

I am a little goat.

The three goats all loved to eat grass.

They ate grass all day long on the hill. But they never crossed the bridge to eat the grass on the other side.

They never crossed the bridge because the Troll lived under the bridge.

The Troll was very bad. He ate anyone who dared to cross his bridge.

One day the little Billy Goat Gruff looked at the green, green grass on the other side of the bridge.

"I'm not scared of a silly old Troll," he said.

"I'm going to cross the bridge."

"Me too," said the middle-sized Billy Goat Gruff.

"And me," said the big Billy Goat Gruff.

"You go first. It was your idea," said the big Billy Goat Gruff to the little Billy Goat Gruff.

Trip, trap, trip, trip, trap!

So the little Billy Goat Gruff set off across the bridge.

Trip, trap, trip, trip, trap went his hooves.

"Who is that trip-trapping over my bridge?" roared the Troll.

"It's only me!" said the little Billy Goat Gruff. "I'm going to eat the green, green grass on the other side of the bridge."

"Oh no, you're not!" roared the Troll. "I'm going to eat you up!"

"But I am just little," said the little Billy Goat Gruff. "Wait until my middle-sized brother comes across. He is far bigger than me." "Very well!" said the Troll.

So the little Billy Goat Gruff crossed the bridge.
Soon he was eating the green, green grass.

Next, the middle-sized Billy Goat Gruff crossed the bridge.

"Who is that trip-trapping over my bridge?" roared the Troll.

"It's only me!" said the middle-sized Billy Goat Gruff. "I am going to eat the green, green grass on the other side of the bridge."

"Oh no, you're not!" roared the Troll. "I'm going to eat you up!"

I'm going to eat you up!

"But I am just middle-sized," said the middle-sized Billy Goat Gruff. "Wait until my big brother comes across. He is far bigger than me."
"Very well!" said the Troll.

And don't come back!

So the middle-sized Billy Goat Gruff crossed the bridge. Soon he was eating the green, green grass.

Next the big Billy Goat Gruff crossed the bridge.

Quake! Shake! Rumble!

"Who is that trip-trapping over my bridge?" roared the Troll.

"It's only me!" said the big Billy Goat Gruff. "I'm going to eat the green, green grass on the other side of the bridge."

"Oh no, you're not!" roared the Troll. "I'm going to eat you up!"

I'm going to eat you up!

The Troll jumped onto the bridge.

The big Billy Goat Gruff lowered his horns and charged.

Crash! The big Billy Goat Gruff banged into the Troll. The Troll flew into the air. Splash! He fell into the water.

Take that!

Crash!
Splash!

The big Billy Goat Gruff skipped over the bridge.

Soon he was eating the green, green grass.

And the ugly Troll was never seen again.

Hooray!

27

Read and Say

How many of these words can you say?
The pictures will help you. Look back in your book
and see if you can find the words in the story.

big goat

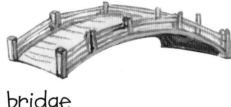

bridge

grass

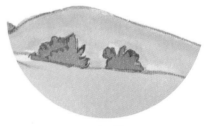

hill

horns

hooves

little goat

middle-sized goat

Troll

water

29

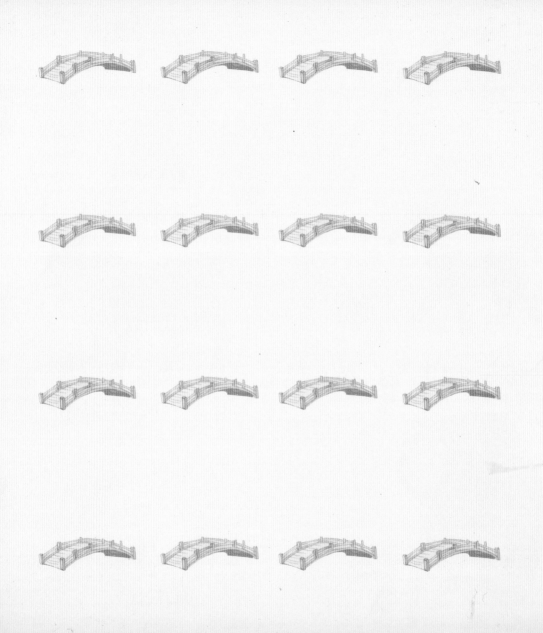